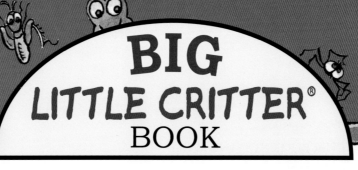

BIG
LITTLE CRITTER®
BOOK

STAYING WELL

THIS IS MY BODY 3

TAKING CARE OF MOM 27

I WAS SO SICK 51

THE LOOSE TOOTH 75

BY GINA AND MERCER MAYER

Printed in China
46732802 2014

Published by FastPencil PREMIERE
307 Orchard City Drive, Suite 210, Campbell CA 95008
Premiere.FastPencil.com

THIS IS MY BODY

BY GINA AND MERCER MAYER

This is my body. It has different parts.
They all work together.

This is my fur. It keeps me warm,
especially in the wintertime.

When my fur gets too long, my mom takes me
to the barber for a furcut. If I sit really still, I
get a special treat.

These are my eyes.
They help me to see.

I use them to see
a little green worm . . .

to see a big tree . . .

and to see my dad
when he comes home
from work. "Hi, Dad!"

Sometimes I have to use my eyes
to watch my little brother. I don't like
to use them for that, though.

These are my ears.
They help me to hear.

I can hear when my dog barks.
That means someone's here.

I can also hear when my mom
asks me to clean my room.
Then I wish I didn't hear so well.

11

This is my nose.
It helps me to smell.

I can smell
Mom's perfume.

ZZZZZ

12

I can smell
my shampoo.

I can smell when my dog
has been playing with
a skunk! Ugh!

This is my mouth.

I use it to eat and to talk.
Dad says I talk all the time.
I guess I just have a lot to say.

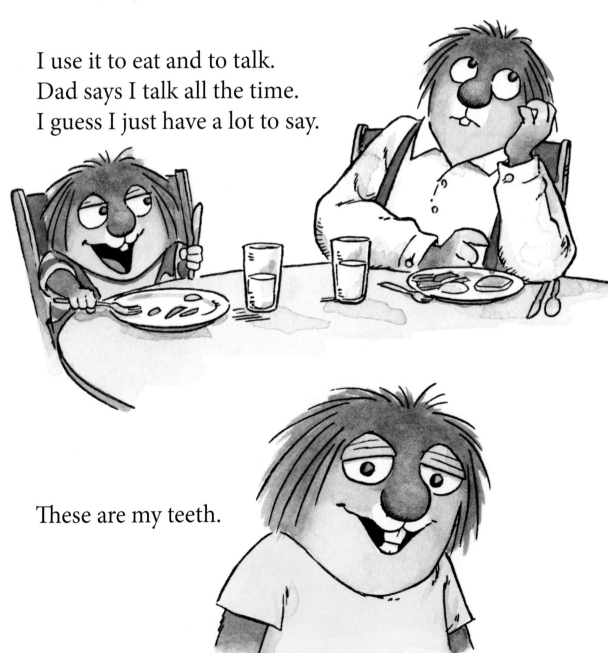

These are my teeth.

They help me to chew
things I like . . .

and sometimes things
I don't really like.

I brush my teeth every night
to keep them clean.

15

This is my tummy.

This is where the food goes after I eat.

Sometimes if I eat too much sweet stuff
I get a tummy ache. That's why Mom
won't let me eat a whole bag of cookies.

These are my arms and hands.
I use them all the time.

They help me to turn
cartwheels . . .

to steer my bike . . .

and to turn pages of a book.

When I lasso a dinosaur, they help me
tie him up. They help me do
just about everything.

Especially take my toys back from my sister.

These are my elbows.

I use them to prop up my head
when I'm sleepy.

These are my legs
and feet.

I use them to walk.

. . . and climb.

When my sister is bothering me,
I use my legs and feet to run away from her.

23

These are my knees.
They help my legs bend.

When I fall down, my knees
always get banged up.

All the parts of my body work together
so I can do anything I want.

Everyone's body looks different,
but I think that's what makes us all special.

TAKING CARE OF MOM

BY GINA AND MERCER MAYER

Mom was sick. She had a stuffy nose
and a fever.
She had to stay in bed all day. She couldn't
even take us to the playground.

28

29

Dad had to go to work, so Grandma
came to pick up my baby brother.
Grandma said my sister and I
should go to her house, too.

But we didn't want to. We wanted to
stay home and take care of Mom.
Grandma said, "All right, but you have
to let your mother rest."

We were really careful not to bother mom.

We got dressed by ourselves.

We fixed our own breakfast.

I found my favorite game
without asking for help.

I even opened a bag of chips by myself.

We only bothered Mom when it was really important—like when my sister spilled the jar of pickles.

We took Mom some juice when we thought she might be thirsty. We only spilled a little bit on her bed.

We fixed Mom a sandwich for lunch.
We didn't know what kind she would want,
so we put a little of everything on it.

We tried to keep the puppy off her bed.
He sure was sneaky though.

39

We took my mom a hot water bottle to
keep her warm. But it leaked a little.

And we brought her another box of tissues. Her nose was so red.

We even cleaned up a little bit.

I washed the dishes.

My sister picked up some of the toys.

43

Then we decided to go outside and play.
We put on our coats and hats.

We told Mom we would be outside
in case she needed us.

We played outside
all afternoon.

When we came back in. Mom looked like she was feeling a little better.

Mom was better because we took such good care of her. Dad said he thought so, too.

Taking care of Mom was fun.

But I like it a lot better
when she takes care of us.

50

I WAS SO SICK

BY GINA AND MERCER MAYER

Last night I woke up with a tummy ache.
I called Mom. She said I had a fever.

She put a cool washcloth on my head and
rubbed my tummy. I was so sick.

Mom sat beside my bed and held
my hand all night.

In the morning I was still sick. I didn't have to go to school, but even that didn't make me happy. I'd rather go to school than be so sick.

Mom said, "We need to go to the doctor to get some medicine for your tummy."

I didn't want to go to the doctor, but I wanted
to feel better. So I was brave.

There were lots of toys at the doctor's office,
but I was so sick I didn't play with any of them.

A pretty nurse took us to a room. I sat on a bed covered with paper.

Then the doctor came in. He had big ears. But he had a nice smile.

He asked the nurse to take my temperature. I only had a little fever.

He put a stick in my mouth and told me to say, "Aahh." I thought that was weird.

Then he listened to my heart. He let me listen. It sounded like a drum.

He looked into my ears. He let me look into his ears.

Then he pushed on my tummy. It didn't even hurt.

63

The doctor gave my mom a prescription for some medicine. He said it would make my tummy as good as new.

He shook my hand. "You were a very good patient,"
he said.
I got a big red balloon.

We went to the drugstore to get my medicine.
I was so sick, I forgot to ask for a new toy.

When we got home, Mom made me take my
medicine. Yuck!

Then I lay down on the couch to watch cartoons.
I went to sleep by accident.

When I woke up, I started to cry because I had missed my cartoons.

But my tummy felt better.
That doctor was so smart!

When Dad came home, I told him all about the
doctor and the pretty nurse.
"You're such a brave critter," he said.

Then he read me a story and
put me to bed.

Dad says I'll probably be all better tomorrow.
Boy, I sure hope so.

THE LOOSE TOOTH

BY GINA AND MERCER MAYER

When I bit into a peach, I felt
my tooth wiggle. I didn't know
teeth could wiggle.
I yelled for Mom and Dad.

Mom said, "When little critters get bigger,
their baby teeth get loose and come out."

I started to cry. I didn't want to
lose my teeth. Then I wouldn't be able to eat.
Mom said, "You get big teeth in place
of the little ones."

Dad said, "When you lose your tooth, put it under your pillow. Then when you wake up, you'll find a surprise from the Tooth Fairy."

That made me feel a lot better.
Dad showed me how to wiggle my tooth.
He said, "Wiggling your tooth may make
it come out faster."

I wiggled my tooth in front of the mirror.

I wiggled my tooth while I was doing homework.

I wiggled my tooth while I was in my clubhouse.

I wiggled my tooth when
I was in the bathtub.

I even let my little sister
wiggle my tooth.

But it still didn't come out.

At my Little League® baseball game, I showed my friends my loose tooth. One of my friends said he got baseball cards under his pillow when he lost his tooth.

When it was my turn at bat,
I hit the ball really hard.
It was a home run!

When I slid into home, I slammed
right into the catcher.

The coach came over to see if we were okay.
He noticed my tooth was missing.
We found it right beside home plate.

Mom and Dad came over to get me, and I showed them my tooth. My sister laughed "You look funny," she said.

I looked in the mirror. I did look kind of funny.
My sister kept calling me "Snaggletooth."
Dad made her stop.

At dinner it was hard to eat because
my mouth was kind of sore.

And it felt really weird when I brushed my teeth.

Later I tucked my tooth in under my pillow. I went right to sleep. Losing my tooth made me tired.

I dreamed I was in a candy store, but I couldn't eat anything because I didn't have any teeth. It was terrible.

When I woke up, I checked under my pillow.
My tooth was gone. And a whole dollar bill
was in its place.

I think I'll put my dollar in my piggy bank
until the rest of my teeth come out.

Then I'll have lots of dollars and I can buy
anything I want. Well . . . almost anything.